Rod Clement spent his childhood in New Guinea and on the north coast of NSW. After three years of study at Mitchell College in Bathurst, he managed to fail just enough subjects to still get an Associate Diploma in Media Studies. He now combines writing and illustrating children's books with a job as a full-time cartoonist for a major Australian newspaper.

Rod lives in Sydney with his wife and three children.

OTHER BOOKS BY ROD CLEMENT:

WRITTEN AND ILLUSTRATED:

Eyes in Disguise

Counting on Frank

Just Another Ordinary Day

Grandad's Teeth

Frank in Time

Louisa May Pickett's Best Show and Tell

Feathers for Phoebe

ILLUSTRATED:

Snail Mail
written by Hazel Edwards

Edward the Emu
written by Sheena Knowles

Edwina the Emu
written by Sheena Knowles

OLGA the BROLGA

ROD CLEMENT

Angus&Robertson
An imprint of HarperCollins*Children'sBooks*

Angus&Robertson
An imprint of HarperCollins*Children'sBooks*, Australia

First published in Australia in 2002
This edition published in 2005
by HarperCollins*Publishers* Pty Ltd
ABN 36 009 913 517
harpercollins.com.au

HarperCollins*Publishers*
Level 13, 201 Elizabeth Street, Sydney NSW 2000, Australia
Unit D1, 63 Apollo Drive, Rosedale, Auckland 0632, New Zealand
A 53, Sector 57, Noida, UP, India
1 London Bridge Street, London, SE1 9GF, United Kingdom
2 Bloor Street East, 20th floor, Toronto, Ontario M4W 1A8, Canada
195 Broadway, New York NY 10007, USA

National Library of Australia Cataloguing-in-Publication data:

Clement, Rod.
Olga the brolga

For children.
ISBN 978 0 2071 9758 1 (pbk.)
1. Brolga - Juvenile fiction. I. Title.

A823.3

The illustrator used watercolour and coloured inks on paper.
Colour reproduction by Graphic Print Group, Adelaide, South Australia.
Printed by RR Donnelley in China on 128gsm Matt Art.

24 23 22 21 16 17 18 19

To all the great people
at Lucas Gardens School

Olga the brolga was in a terrible mood.

She was whiny and pushy
and downright rude.

She jumped on the table, knocked over the tea.
'Will you dance with me, Dad?
Please, please, dance with me!'
Her father looked cross and straightened his paper.
'I'm having my breakfast,
so no, maybe later.'

'Don't ask me,' said her mum.
'Don't ask me again.
Don't ask me where,
don't ask me when.
Now hop off the table,
dance outside for a while.
Go dance with your friend,
the old crocodile.'

Ellie lay in the sun,
her mouth yawning wide,
her tail in the water
being lapped by the tide.

'Ellie!' cried Olga, giving Ellie a fright.
'Your tummy's too big and your skin's too tight.
You must dance with me,
we'll go jiving and grooving!'

'No!' replied Ellie. 'I'm very happy not moving.
Why don't you ask Joanna Jacana?
I saw her dancing last night
at the Club Tropicana.'

Olga found Joanna tired and sad,
collapsed in a heap on a large lilypad.
Walking on water is hard enough,
but dancing on water — boy, that was tough.

'Let's dance together out here on the marsh,'
Olga honked in a voice both loud and harsh.
'Not today,' said Joanna, barely raising her head,
'maybe tomorrow, when I get out of bed.'

‘I want to dance NOW,
I want to flap, kick and jump!’

‘Well, don’t jump on me!’
said a small brown lump.

Lilly the long-neck popped out her head,
'I'm a turtle not a dance floor,
try a log instead.'

Olga rose from the deep,
feeling wet and dejected.
Her plans for a dance
had been rudely rejected.

Her shouting, her nagging,
had all gone unheeded.
She must try something else
to get what she needed.

Olga stood on one leg
and thought for a while.
Then paused and smiled
a shy little smile.

She danced alone,
slowly at first,
then faster and faster,
till she thought she would burst.

She kicked, she flapped,
she flew through the air.
Everyone passing
stopped to stare.

Olga stayed silent,
she said not a word.
Sometimes it's better
to be seen and not
heard.

Soon a crowd gathered,
they picked up the beat.
There was a shuffling of feathers,
a tapping of feet.

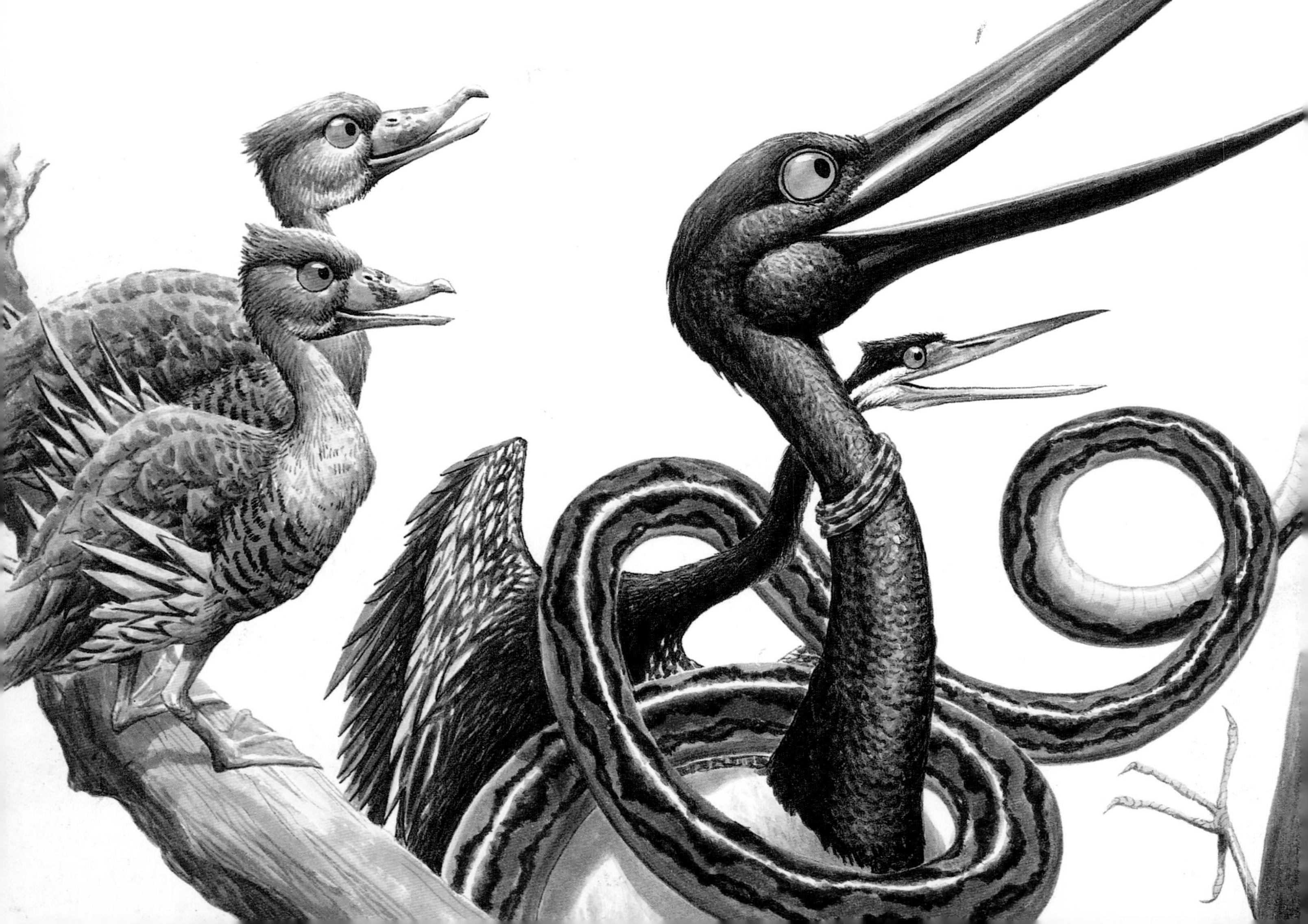

As the whistling ducks whistled
the latest dance tunes,
Olga and friends danced
all afternoon.

When the sun finally set
and darkness descended,
they said their goodbyes
and the dance party ended.

Olga was tired,
but happy at last.
She'd got what she wanted
without having asked.